The

Summer Adventure For GROOT

starts today!
There's so much to see—
no time to delay.

Accept the challenge of this special mission:
Map every planet for your expedition!
I AM GROOOOOT!
THE WHOLE THING IN ONE DAY?! IF YOU SAY SO, BUDDY!
FINISH

The very first stop is well within reach.
Start out your day with a trip to the beach!

Build a sand castle that's second to none,
while your friends kick back and enjoy the sun.

Asgardians *love* to play hide-and-seek.
Be careful with Loki—he tends to peek!

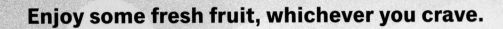

Enjoy some fresh fruit, whichever you crave.

Surf's up on Zenn-La, so let's catch a wave!

Competition can help you hone a new skill.
If you win or lose, keep up the goodwill!

Explore the outdoors by taking a hike . . .

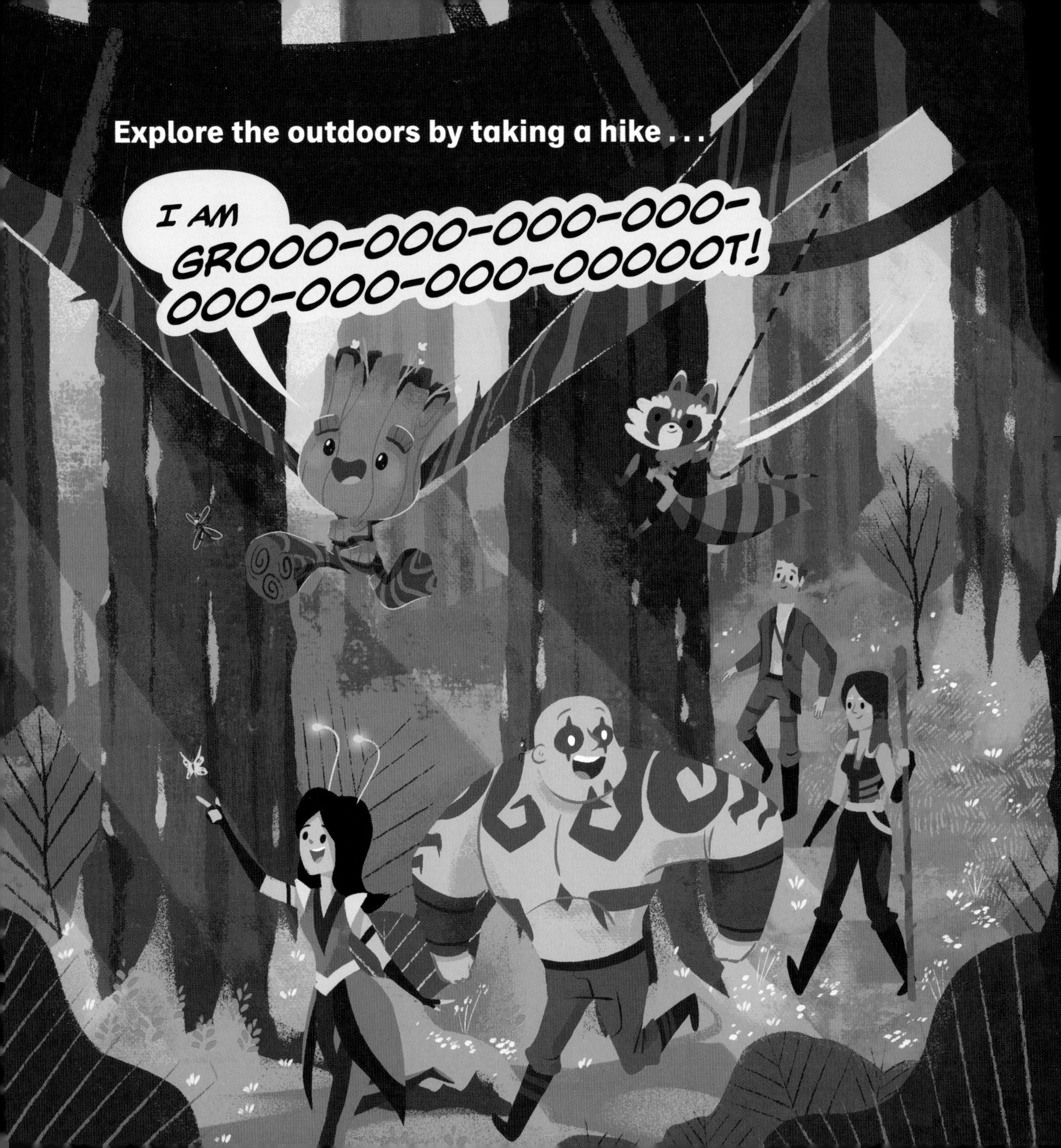

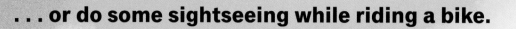

. . . or do some sightseeing while riding a bike.

The galaxy is home to many a creature,
but colorful flowers are Groot's favorite feature.

Up next on the map: the Grand Canyon of Mars.
Explore all its spots lit up by the stars.

As each sun sets, the daylight will fade.

The fireflies dance and glow in the shade.

A nebula flares in the dark of the night . . .

. . . but planets with more than one moon are alight.

The campfire roars, the night is still young!
Don't go home yet—there are songs to be sung.

When the theater's in space,
you can't beat the view.

Dazzling fireworks light up the sky
as the perfect way to bid the day good-bye.

The best part of a fun-filled, long summer day
is getting back home after being away.

Printed in the United States of America

First Edition, April 2021   10 9 8 7 6 5 4 3 2 1

ISBN: 978-1-368-00071-0

FAC-034274-21050

Library of Congress Control Number: 2020937160

Reinforced binding